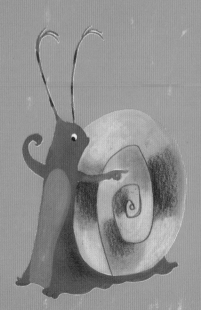

For Harold
Fiona Rempt

For Jeroen
Noëlle Smit

First published by Gottmer in 2006
©Uitgeverij J.H. Gottmer/ H.J.W. Becht bv, Haarlem, The Netherlands; a division of the Gottmer Uitgeversgroep BV.

First American edition published in 2007 by Boxer Books Ltd

Distributed in the United States and Canada by Sterling Publishing Co., Inc.
387 Park Avenue South, New York, NY 10016-8810

First published in Great Britain in 2007 by Boxer Books Limited
www.boxerbooks.com

ISBN 10: 1-905417-52-7
ISBN 13: 978-1-905417-52-0

1 3 5 7 9 10 8 6 4 2

Printed in China

Snail's Birthday Wish

Fiona Rempt

with illustrations by Noëlle Smit

Boxer Books

Today is Snail's birthday. All Snail's forest friends have come to celebrate. There's Beaver and Squirrel, Duck and Mole – and they're bringing balloons and presents for Snail!

Now Frog and Ant have
arrived. Snail's friends are
having lots of fun!
But Snail can't join in.
Snail's not fast enough.

They climb
and splash
and swim.
"Who wants a slice of
my birthday cake?"
asks Snail.

"Make a wish, make a wish!" says Squirrel.
And Snail makes a wish.

Snail wishes he could be as fast
as all his friends.

Then Snail huffs and puffs
and blows out all the candles.

"Present time!" says Duck.
"From all the ducks in the pond."
Snail carefully unwraps Duck's present.
"A chair!" says Snail, a little puzzled.

Next, Ant gives Snail a pretty bag of nails.

The nails are all made from pine needles.

"They are very, very strong." says Ant happily.

Then Beaver proudly tells Snail,
"This is the best wood in the forest.
And I polished it with my teeth, so you
won't find any splinters!"

Now it is Mole's turn to give a present.

"They go on your feet!" Mole says.

"Are they snowshoes?" Snail says to himself.

Snail opens the present from Frog.

"Do I put this on my head?" says Snail.

"I made it from pond weed," says Frog.

"But I'm not telling you what it's for!"

Squirrel has four more presents for Snail.

Squirrel swings them around enthusiastically.

"Here they come!" shouts Squirrel.

"Look out!" says Frog.

"I wonder what they are," thinks Snail.

"Wheels!" says Snail. "Thank you. I don't know what all these presents are for but they are wonderful!"

"The best is yet to come," says Beaver.
"Come on everyone, let's get to work!"
And Snail's friends begin to build something
out of all the presents.

"Happy birthday Snail!" shout Snail's friends.
"It's a car! Whoopee!" shouts Snail.
"My birthday wish came true!"